Scraps of
Old Paper, a Desk
and a Pen

PAT DAVIS

Scraps of Old Paper, a Desk and a Pen
Copyright © 2022 by Pat Davis

All rights reserved. No part of this publication may be reproduced, distributed, or transmitted in any form or by any means, including photocopying, recording, or other electronic or mechanical methods, without the prior written permission of the author, except in the case of brief quotations embodied in critical reviews and certain other non-commercial uses permitted by copyright law.

Tellwell Talent
www.tellwell.ca

ISBN
978-0-2288-6664-0 (Paperback)
978-0-2288-7431-7 (eBook)

Table of Contents

Introduction 1
Target Audience 2
Dedication 3
Holy Spirit 4
House 6
The Ratty Little Cradle 9
Daphne's Prayer 19
The Christmas Pajamas 21
The Card 25
Remind Me, Lord Jesus 27
Jesus, If I Had To 37
Searching 39
Miracle At Mclaren's Creek 41
Jesus Showed Me 47
Nails 50
Lampstand 52
Competition 54
Missing 56
Unwavering 58
Jesus And The Swimmer 60
Jesus Was There 62
Call Out To Jesus 65
Tears From A Pen 68
Epilogue 71

Introduction

Some of this book is a journey of my life without Jesus, but it is mostly my life with our Savior. I always knew of the Lord but didn't follow Him. Yet, He was always in the back of my mind, especially at Christmas, and I always wanted my children to know about Jesus, so I would write fictional stories about Him. Each Christmas was when I would write their anticipated story, it was one of their favorite gifts they looked forward to.

It wasn't until certain events in my life and a friend's witness of the Lord, that I finally asked Jesus into my life for good. I was not sure how the Lord would lead me, especially since I had no real writing abilities. Reading His Word and spending time in prayer with Him, I found myself in awe of who He actually is.

This led to sitting down at my desk to write a collection of fictional poetry and stories of my very real journey with Jesus, inspired by the Holy Spirit. It is not an easy road to travel but the Lord has shown me through beautiful signs and wonders that He is definitely there every step of the way. My hope is that this book will inspire others to give their lives over to Christ to further His Kingdom long after my time here.

Pat Davis

Target Audience

This book is designed for anyone 14 years of age and up who wants his or her life to mean something, as I did—wanting to give something back without knowing how, and without any real skills to do it. I would really love for ordinary people to see and believe—no matter how old, dark, or hopeless they feel—that Jesus reaches in if we open our hearts and minds to Him and finds what we or the world cannot, and turns it into something special. To experience Jesus is a new way of life with no looking back. Look to the future and watch how He creates new abilities that were hidden to feed the hungry soul!

Dedication

This book is dedicated to the Holy Spirit, whose inspiration and guidance made this book possible; my husband and my family, whose constant support and encouragement helped me to keep writing; and to the Gordon Williams Evangelical Association for introducing me to the Holy Spirit to further my spiritual growth in my journey with Jesus Christ. Amen.

Holy Spirit

Your cool wind embraces the restless soul,
Searching for its first love when it was told.
Holy Spirit was there at the beginning of time,
To help birth the Son Jesus who was to die.
Creating the world at the Lord's command,
Breathing life into its first woman and its first man.
You welcomed the faithfulness of all the old prophets,
And carry out the duties of the Lord's precious promises.
Holy Spirit offers love and life-giving conviction,
Given by the Son Jesus, for all of man's afflictions.
Let the power of Your love continually shine through,
Guide us to the Father's will, to show us what to do.
Holy Spirit, You hold the keys of the Lord to our future,
Until the day we are prayerful and fully mature.
We thank You for all the unseen work that You possess,
Thank You for the gifts of the Lord in quietness.
We try to capture the lesson of Your still, small voice,
Accordingly to Your leading, we rejoice!
Each revelation by You to us is given,
By God the Father, "Who art in heaven."
Our prayers are Yours to intercede,
Without You, Holy Spirit, they could never be.
Holy Spirit, He gently guides my pen,
Sits with me quietly at my desk.

Helps me to write stories that He wants said,
While I contemplate His Word that is in my head.
Of signs and wonders and all that I have seen.
All through His Word is where I've been.
Holy Spirit shows the way to Jesus our Lord,
When the enemy of our spirit comes for war.
No matter what, You're always there,
Giving us protection when we become scared.
It is now, Holy Spirit, we need You more than ever,
The enemy closing in thinks he's so clever.
Not understanding, we have You as our weapon,
One of the reasons he lost by Your Word, I would reckon.
The world she spins in and out of control,
Sometimes it's hard for Christians to be bold.
But with Your strength, Holy Spirit, we persevere,
Help us look to the Lord Jesus, and always hold Him dear.
Amen!

House

There was an old house in ruin and old paint,
Around it an iron fence locked by chains and sealed gate.
Inside lie scraps of old paper, a desk and a pen,
Surrounded in blackened darkness, keeping its occupant within.
Its frame is full of patches and full of shattered holes,
How could this have happened?
No one really knows.
No more could it hold back its bursting at the seams,
Its voice cries out in silent, tormented, painful screams.
Its foundation had cracked, neglected over years,
Its taps drip with sorrow and rivers of endless tears.
Thick webs of painful memories were its only company,
Papering all its walls that no one ever sees.
Its hearth which burned bright, now burns only cold,
While shivers of fears and anxieties run down its empty halls.
The windows reflect nothing, couldn't see through their panes,
The door welded shut; its threshold bears a name.
No one dared to enter its maze of senseless rooms,
While whispers of mocking laughter engulf its eerie tombs.
The house had fallen apart, surely to be condemned,

While the voice of fate and deceit decide its final end.
There's nothing to be done; it's hopeless to repair.
The house barely standing, its name is called Depression
  and Despair.
"Savior," a voice calls from the deep halls of distress,
"Save me from this deteriorating wrecking ball of death."
Suddenly the doors fling open and there a figure stands,
He's come to save the house, with His Spirit close at
  hand.
He was blessed Jesus, King of Kings, Lord of Lords,
He swung the broken chains and smashed the welded
  door.
Crying tears of mercy at what this house endured,
He brought this house Salvation that was true and sure.
Jesus planted seeds in the ground that was once
  only mud,
The seeds grow leaves of life and trees of perfect love.
With all of Heaven's tools Jesus had on hand,
Starting with its roof, the renovations began.
He cleansed the rooms of filth, hidden by great loss,
By the blood He shed upon that painful cross.
The commanding thunderous whispers of His Holy
  breath,
Blew away despair and thoughts of certain death,
His Light shattered darkness from inside and out,
Freeing the enslaved captive with the sword of His
  mouth.
Jesus lifted its burdened corners that were surely to fall,
Ordered fear and anxiety out from the empty halls.
He cut through thickened webs of painful memories,

Replacing the voice of torment with compassion and His peace.
He blew out the taps of sorrow, turned off the dripping tears,
They run with Living Waters, pure and crystal clear.
He polished the lifeless windows with a corner of His robe,
And now looking through them are smiles from the Holy Ghost.
The crumbling foundation Jesus secured with His love,
Injecting joy and happiness approved from above.
Tearing down the fence, He unlocked the sealed gate,
Jesus gave this old house a coat of Heaven's paint!
The doors of love now open, welcoming others to come in,
To praise and worship Jesus, who took away its pain and scrubbed it from its sins.
The house has now bowed down to the Holy King of Kings,
Amazing grace and other hymns, the grateful house now sings.
The house is now finely furnished,
With gifts of gold paper, desk, and pen,
Jesus renamed the house Hallelujah and Amen.

The Ratty Little Cradle

It was getting near to Christmas this year and Anna had been decorating her house. Julie and her two grandchildren would be spending Christmas with her this year! It had been quite a while since Anna had Julie and Kirsten home for Christmas, as the children were now getting older and Kirsten had moved five hours away from Anna and Mike. Life had been difficult for Julie in the last few years: her marriage had broken up, and Julie had to move in with Anna until she could find a place for her and the children. Things were rapidly changing and it had been especially difficult for Julie; everything was so expensive and she was becoming discouraged with her situation. Now both women had given themselves over to the Lord and tried as they could to have faith that the Lord would help them out.

"I'm so tired of struggling, Mom," said Julie. "I don't have any Christmas spirit at all!"

"Don't worry," said Anna, trying to reassure her daughter. "The Lord will come through. He won't abandon you, trust Him."

With tear filled eyes, Julie in her desperation, said, "Really? Is He, really? I'm so sick of everybody else seeming to get along and have everything they want, while I'm barely hanging on; it must be nice that these people have parents who buy them everything so they don't have to worry," a discouraged Julie retorted.

"Yes, Julie, but remember, what they don't have is the Lord," Anna reminded her daughter.

Very quickly, Julie said quietly, "Yes, you're right, Mom," and walked away.

Anna's heart broke for her daughter. She wanted so much to help her but there was only so much she could do and had to leave Julie in the Lord's hands. Anna also, at times, had trouble trusting the Lord, just as Julie did, but that incident at the shelter years ago changed Anna's heart forever. At one time Anna was filled with bitterness and want herself, but it wasn't something she ever shared with anyone, not even Mike, her husband, as he did his best to look after everyone and Anna loved him for it.

Early the next morning, Anna was getting out the last of her Christmas decorations for her front porch when her friend Carol showed up.

"Looks beautiful, Anna, but are you really going to put out that ratty cradle again?"

"Yes," said Anna. "I'm hoping to give it to Julie for Christmas this year!"

"Oh, you can't be serious, Anna," said Carol. "I mean... I mean, Anna, look at it." As Anna looked adoringly at the cradle, Carol said, "Anna, why don't you have Rick from the church fix it up for you, at least?"

Anna thanked her friend for the idea, but she wanted to give it to Julie just as it was when it was given to her. After finishing with the decorations and her visit with her friend, Anna went in to make coffee for both her and Julie, who had earnestly been looking for work and a home. It was late afternoon and Anna as tired from the business of getting things ready for Christmas. She wanted to make it extra special for Julie. Thinking of that cradle, she could hardly wait to give it to her daughter. As she lay resting, her mind went back in time to the shelter where she had once volunteered.

She remembered how she saw people walking past the shelter, with lots of shopping bags full of gifts, hurrying to get back to their homes to get them wrapped. Anna, feeling depressed, shrugged it off and got back to work to help other families who were worse off than her, and this made her feel somewhat better. Halfway through her shift, a young man walked in, a new volunteer. Anna was to train him and show him the ropes.

"Hi," he said with a smile that could warm any heart, "my name is Jimmy. You're Anna? They told me I was supposed to come see you and you would show me what needs to be done."

Anna couldn't believe that such a nice young man would want to work in a place like a shelter when there were so many other opportunities for people of his age. *Hmm,* she thought to herself, *unusual, since young volunteers are hard to find.* But, grateful for the help, she proceeded to show him around and told him his job would be to wash the dishes. Jimmy was glad for the job of doing the dishes, as washing up was one of his many talents! *Cheek!* Anna thought to herself, but laughed at his tenacity; it was good to laugh, as there was very little of it at the shelter. She was quite surprised at how well Jimmy had taken to his job and the people wholeheartedly. He had fit in better than other volunteers who had come and gone.

One afternoon, they had finished their work early and Anna asked Jimmy if he would like to grab some lunch, as neither one had eaten. She made them some sandwiches and hot chocolate, which they both enjoyed. As she watched him, she was curious, and wanted to know more about him.

"Jimmy," she said, looking squarely at him, "where do you live?'

"Oh," he said, "I live with my father. I've given the address many times to people but they seem to have a hard time finding it." But he didn't tell Anna where he lived. Obviously, he didn't want to share this part of himself, so Anna didn't push the question any further; instead, he asked her a question.

"So how long have you been volunteering here?"

"Well, just a few years, not very long. I'm hoping to add to my resume so I can find a better job," she answered.

"You're not happy with the job you have already? he asked.

"Well, no," she answered. "Mike and I are just barely making ends meet, and I'm tired of always struggling," she said bitterly. Anna felt bad for complaining about her situation, but it bothered her that she couldn't do more.

"So, you're married? Any kids? "Jimmy asked.

"No, not yet, maybe after I get a better job. Mike wants kids but I don't, not until I get a good paying job and a better house to raise them in."

"Well, maybe it will happen for you." With that, they ended their conversation and got back to work preparing dinner. When the dinner hour was over and the last of the dishes were done, Jimmy swept the floors while Anna checked that all the food was put away and then turned out the lights. Jimmy was at the door waiting for her and she asked him if he needed a ride home, but Jimmy was quick to decline. As she turned to say goodbye, he had already gone.

There was something about Jimmy that Anna really liked, as did the other volunteers, but what, specifically, was it? He appeared to be like any young man his age, a little reckless maybe, but there was a genuineness to him.

Back home, Anna was happy to greet her husband who had been waiting at the door for her. She thought to herself, if anything made her happy, it was his smiling face as he greeted her with a hug. It was Christmas and she and Mike did not have gifts to give to one another but they were happy, they were together.

Months went by. It was springtime, and Jimmy explained to Anna that he had to be away for a while, but that he would be back in the early fall to help with the Christmas rush, as this was a busy time for the shelter. One day, Anna was serving food when suddenly she felt very ill and fainted. She was taken to the hospital, where she found, she was going to have a baby!

"Oh no, Mike!" she exclaimed with shock. "We said not until we got better jobs!" But Mike reassured her that things would be okay and he would make sure they were looked after. The look of joy in Mike's eyes melted her heart and soon she was happy with the idea. Months passed and, as promised, Jimmy returned and was overjoyed for Anna and Mike at hearing their happy news. Jimmy looked tired but in good spirits.

One day, Jimmy asked Anna a question. He asked her if she knew Jesus as her Savior. Shocked by his question, Anna uncomfortably said no, that it was not something she believed in. "Anna, "he said, "would you like to know Him?" My father told me all about Him and it's a fascinating story!"

"Well, I don't know, Jimmy, we have a lot of work to do," she said sheepishly.

"Tell you what," said Jimmy. "I can pick up some extra hours here and help out more. After all, you are going to have a baby, you need the help. Then I'll make you lunch and we can chat . . . what do you think?"

"Well," said Anna reluctantly, "I do need the help, and what have I got to lose?" "Absolutely nothing," said Jimmy. "He loves you so much."

Anna was feeling a little down and upon hearing Jimmy say this, surprisingly, it picked up her spirits.

Every day after that, Jimmy brought his Bible and told Anna all about Jesus.

"Oh, Jimmy," said Anna, "The stories are wonderful but I don't think I'm ready. Although maybe after I have my baby, I will be."

Jimmy, with an understanding look, didn't press the issue any further.

One evening, two days before Christmas, Jimmy had left the shelter early and promised to come back before closing. Anna had let him go early as he had earned it and she would finish up. After a few hours, there was a knock on the door of the shelter, and Anna could see Jimmy struggling with what looked like a cradle.

"It's a bit ratty," said Jimmy. "My Father built it for me before I was born. I thought you might like to have it, since it seems that you could use it for your baby girl. My Father told me to give it to you and Mike. Call it our Christmas gift to you both."

"Oh, Jimmy . . . thank you so much!" said Anna.

"Are you celebrating Christmas this year?" he asked.

"No, Jimmy, we just can't afford it," she said bitterly. "I actually hate Christmas—I just want it to be over! But thank you again, and please thank your father, also, for the cradle. I'm sorry I have nothing for you, Jimmy." Anna said this last bit sadly, as Jimmy proceeded to put the cradle in the car.

"That's okay, Anna. Just knowing you and Mike is enough, but just get to know me a little better, okay?"

"Okay, Jimmy." Just as she had gotten into her car, Anna realized she hadn't told him she was having a girl, and what did he mean, "get to know him"? As she turned to ask him how he knew she was having a girl, fear gripped Anna's heart!

"Jimmy! What's wrong? Somebody, help!" she screamed. Jimmy's face was wracked with pain and blood was everywhere! Soon an ambulance was on the way to take Jimmy to the hospital. Mike had arrived to take care of Anna and wanted to take her home.

"No, Mike!" Anna cried. "I'm not leaving him."

"Where is he?" asked Mike, worried about Anna and the baby.

"He's in with the doctors—, they're working on him. I don't know how to get in touch with his father. There is no phone number or address!"

"Shush, Anna, he'll be okay. What happened?"

Anna, shaken, had told Mike how Jimmy had suddenly started bleeding everywhere and with a horrible look of pain, he just suddenly fell to the ground, and no matter what the paramedics did, they could not stop the bleeding. Soon the doctors came out and explained there was nothing they could do for Jimmy. They seemed to think he had been shot or stabbed. It was unclear, as there didn't appear to be any bullets left in his body, so they couldn't tell for sure, but his arteries sustained irreparable damage. There was no clear explanation for his injuries.

The police asked Anna a whole bunch of questions: Had she heard any shots? Did Jimmy have any enemies? etc. The doctor told Anna and Mike that Jimmy wanted to see them, which the doctor had allowed since no family could be located. Anna sat on a chair beside Jimmy's bed, crying, while Mike held his hand on his other side. Jimmy had come to be like one of the family, and they both loved him.

"Mike," Anna said, "we have to pray. Maybe this Jesus that Jimmy talks about will save him." Mike understood, as Anna had shared with her husband what Jimmy had told her about Jesus. "I don't know how to pray, Mike," Anna said.

Suddenly, Jimmy spoke softly and said, "Just be yourselves and talk to Him like you have Me."

"Oh, Jimmy!" Anna cried. "Please hold on . . . we are trying to find your Father."

"Anna, He is here with me now," said Jimmy.

After a short, sorrowful pause, Mike whispered, "Anna, he's delirious," and they knelt before the Lord to ask Him to save Jimmy. They prayed hard, and as they did, they noticed something strange happening: Jimmy was not Jimmy anymore. His face was obscured so they couldn't see it, but they could see the hole in His side and hands.

"Anna," He said, "do not be afraid. I, the Lord your God, have offered you a gift, because you have prayed and believed My Son, I have blessed you. You will give birth in two days to a daughter and she will be blessed, only she will not know it until later in life."

"Jesus?" said Anna in shock. "Is it really You?"

Both she and Mike fell into unconsciousness. The Lord explained in the Spirit to Anna and Mike that He knew their hearts but needed to take measures to bring them to Him, and they did: two days later, Julie was born. Anna put Julie in the cradle the Lord had given them, on which were engraved the words, "My grace is sufficient. Love, Jesus." Anna never again complained of what she didn't have; she learned that His grace was sufficient and sought to serve the Lord. Mike did the same. Over the years they came to understand the vision the Lord had given them. Julie and Mike never had an encounter with the Lord like that again; only in faith did they believe. Was it a dream? They didn't know but never questioned what they saw.

Anna awoke from her sleep and surprised at the time said, "Oh my goodness! I have slept a long time; I must hurry and get the rest of my chores done."

Soon it was Christmas and Anna gave Julie the cradle and told her the story of her and Mike's encounter with Jesus. Mike, Anna's husband, had been with the Lord for a few years now.

"Mom, why didn't you tell me this before?" Julie asked, astonished at what she'd heard. Anna told her that just before the time of her birth, the Lord told Anna she would know when she was to pass the cradle on to Julie and tell of this Divine encounter with Him, and this Christmas was the time. Julie never again complained about Christmas or what she didn't have as she, too, learned His grace was indeed sufficient!

Anna got her job the following year and later remarried. Julie was now seven months along and waiting to use the "ratty little cradle" Anna gave her for her own child. Later, Kirsten, her sister, would use it and learn the story from Julie, who was now serving the Lord. Anna, in the meantime, met her "Jimmy Jesus" the Lord once more: He took her home to be with Him and Mike forever.

The end

To my loving daughter Judy, who inspired this story through the power of the Holy Spirit. Amen.

Daphne's Prayer

"Hurry up, Jimmy! We have to hurry in case we miss Him!"

"Whew! Okay, we have to get on our knees, Jimmy."

That's what they said at Jesus' house.

"Hello, Jesus, my name is Daphne and this is my brother Jimmy. We were at Your house today. It was really nice and we didn't let anyone see us peeking, but we heard the man say that You are our Father. Well, we wanted to know, Jimmy and me, if You would be our Father. We have none, and we have no mother—we are what they call orphans. Daddy left us a long time ago, and Mommy got sick and she left too! We didn't understand what they meant when they told us she wasn't coming back.

"The man at Your house said that people go to Heaven when they leave and don't come back to us. I don't understand, Jesus. Why, when we need a daddy and a mommy? Jesus, we live alone on the street and it's awful bad! The man at Your house said that when we call on Your name, You would come fast. I can't remember the right way he said it, but that You would save us. You see, we have no one to look after us; we are afraid and hide every night from people. They scare us bad, and so we run fast to get away.

"You see, Jesus, Jimmy . . . I think he's sick and I don't know what to do. He can't run fast anymore, I think because we don't have any food except what we can get from the farmer. We are sorry. We don't mean to take stuff, but we are so hungry! The man at Your house said many wonderful things about you. He said You were kind and loved little children! Jesus, is that true? That you love us? He said you came to the earth from Heaven to die on a cross and them went back to Heaven so we could go too!

"Oh, Jesus! Jimmy and I went and washed up as best we could, so we could wait for You to come and get us. We promise we won't take stuff, or run away, and we'll help out with other children just like us that You have in heaven—that's if You want us. It's okay, Jesus. We know You must be very busy, so Jimmy and I will wait right here where no one can see us!

"Jesus we're getting so tired . . . is it okay if Jimmy and I sleep while we wait for You to take us to Heaven? The man said we wouldn't be sick, or hungry, or cold—that You would make supper for us! Thank you, Jesus."

It was at that moment the Lord came to take Daphne and Jimmy. He picked them up lovingly in His arms, taking them home to glory! Now they are with their Father in Heaven, not orphans anymore, and yes, they are cared for. Never afraid, sick or cold and yes, they are at the Lord's Table, which He Himself prepared!

Matthew 19:14

"Suffer the little children to come unto Me."
+In Christ Amen+

The Christmas Pajamas

A very long time ago, a little girl was born. She was to be named Anna. As a baby, Anna did not know that she was born into the world with very little. She had a lot of other siblings and her parents struggled to keep food on the table; her mother always had faith that God would always help to provide for them, explaining that as long as there were leftovers, there was room for one more, and so the family grew to eleven children. Anna was the middle child, and a very inquisitive child, always wondering about everything in her world. But she was too young to understand that they were very poor.

One Christmas Eve, Anna had attended church with her family, and the reverend was giving a sermon about the birth of Jesus. Anna was not quite able to understand everything the reverend was talking about, like "Mary wrapped the baby in swaddling clothes."

She whispered to her father, "Daddy, what does swaddling clothes mean?"

Not wanting to disturb the service, her father leaned over quietly and said, "They are Jesus's Christmas pajamas!"

Hmm, thought Anna quietly. *He must be really important to have Christmas pajamas!* She asked her father, "Daddy, do I have Christmas pajamas?"

"No, Anna," he replied, not understanding what she was really asking him.

Later on, that evening, while her father was tucking all of the children into bed, Anna remembered what her father had said about the Christmas pajamas and asked him if she could have Christmas pajamas like Jesus.

"Well," said her father, in terms he thought she could understand, "Jesus was a very special boy, and only He could have Christmas pajamas, because He was the Son of God. But if you're really good, maybe next year you can have some just like Jesus!"

Soon Anna fell asleep, thinking that she would try to be as good as Jesus to get those special pajamas!

Year after year, Anna tried hard to be as good as Jesus, always asking her father, "Will I get my Christmas pajamas this year?" and each time the answer was the same, and sadly, each time Anna thought she had failed. Eventually, Anna grew up and realized that she and her family were different than other families and she stopped asking for them. Anna had grown into womanhood and forgot all about the Christmas pajamas and why she wanted them; however, she did not forget about that special boy named Jesus who got to have those special pajamas.

Anna grew up hard, filled with disappointment, fear and loneliness; she believed she could never measure up to that boy, Jesus, and was resentful of Him. Yet in her heart, especially at Christmas, she could feel His presence, almost as if He was calling to her. Anna never realized how much she really loved Jesus, but with all of her failings, she foolishly accepted the fact that from what she understood, she would never be good enough to accept Him into her life. How could she? She was bitter as life seemed so hard for her.

Time went on. Anna eventually married and was blessed with a baby girl named Julie. Having Julie changed Anna forever: she had so much joy over Julie that she didn't feel all the pain anymore; her heart was filled to the brim with love for her baby daughter. She still thought of Jesus and prayed to Him from time to time.

It was to be Anna's first Christmas with her daughter Julie, when it suddenly came back to her: her childhood wish to have Christmas pajamas. Not having much herself, Anna thought she would always make sure her baby daughter would have Christmas pajamas, would always know she was good—just like Jesus—because to Anna, she was!

Nearly ten years had passed and Anna had yet another baby girl named Kirsten, whom she loved just as much as her firstborn, and again Anna was truly happy with her life, not believing her two children could make her feel this way, again finding peace in the world! Every Christmas, Anna would give her children their Christmas pajamas, but she never told them why they were so special. It wasn't until years later that her children would find out why.

By then, Anna's father had passed. She missed him, especially at Christmas, because even though they didn't have much, he did his best to make Christmas special. For Anna and her girls, the gifting of pajamas became tradition and they were always given on the eve of the birth of Jesus. In what seemed like such a short time, Anna watched her two daughters grow into women and have children of their own, which made Anna a grandmother of four. Anna sat quietly, proudly watching her two daughters nurturing their children and wished again that she could be that good, like her daughters.

The years were passing by faster than ever before. Anna looked in the mirror and watched as every wrinkle on her face appeared faster and became more pronounced. Anna soon realized she was old and yet another Christmas was coming. She went through everyone's list to get what he or she wished for, but the one thing she would not forget to give was their Christmas pajamas: they had to be the first to get.

It was Christmas Eve, and Anna, not realizing she was in the hospital, was so happy to see her children and grandchildren, and to her amazement, her father! Anna asked her father, "Will I get my pajamas tonight?"

Jesus stepped forward and said, "Yes, Anna, I have them right here."

Amen.

The Card

The old man was walking one bright sunny day,
With always a smile, he went on his way.
His clothes rather raggedy, dirty and torn,
His coat was full of holes, and terribly worn.
He was without skills, not even a home,
Each day he walked; He was always alone.
All that he had was a worn-out old card,
One that he carried, close to his heart.
As he walked, he asked only for a pen,
"Jesus loves you," was all he said.
People laughed and pushed him aside,
Pulling out the card, he'd just smile.
"Get out of here," the people mocked,
Whispering contempt as he walked.
Once in a while he'd get a dollar,
"Go get a bath!" people would holler.
He tried to look as best he could,
They'd nothing to fear; he was good.
His gleaming smile begged for people to listen,
His eyes if you looked, they would glisten.
Where was he from, what was his name?
The homeless, you see, were all the same.
Each night he walked to where he slept on the street,
Not a word of discontent would he speak.

Lovingly he remembered the events of the day,
While trying to keep warm on the street where he laid.
With tear-filled eyes he groaned and he wept,
With the card in his pocket, he closely kept.
Today he didn't show for his daily walk,
"Where is he?" people wondered, as they talked.
Then into the crowd a pastor stepped,
Clutching the card, as he too wept.
"On this card," the pastor read,
"Are the names of every man, woman and child,
That the old man had compiled.
And this it what it says,
'Father forgive them for they know not what they do.'
I love them all, take me instead!"

Amen and Amen!

Remind Me, Lord Jesus

Remind me, Lord Jesus, thank You, when the alarm clock rings this morning, to recall to memory that it's really your wake-up call to Salvation.

Remind me, Lord Jesus, thank You, when I begin my day, to recall to memory in Your Word, John 1:1-2: "In the beginning was the Word, and the Word was with God, and the Word was God."

Remind me, Lord Jesus, thank You, to recall to memory as I step into the shower the warmth of the water that makes me ponder the warmth of Your Spirit which resides in me, warming my once cold soul.

Remind me, Lord Jesus, thank You, as it washes away down the drain, to recall to memory Your blood that washed away my sins.

Remind me, Lord Jesus, thank You, to recall to memory as I'm putting on my makeup that with You, I don't have to; You take me as I am.

Remind me, Lord Jesus, thank You, to recall to memory as I dress for the day that in Your Word it says to put on the full armor of God.

Remind me, Lord Jesus, thank You, to recall to memory as I pour a cup of coffee while reading Your Word: You poured for me Your Holy Spirit.

Remind me, Lord Jesus, thank You, as I eat a piece of toast, to recall to memory in Your Word, one of the verses of the Lord's Prayer: "Give us this day our daily bread."

Remind me, Lord Jesus, thank You, that as I look outside and see that it is raining, to recall to memory in Your Word how Mary Magdalene anointed Your feet with her tears.

Remind me, Lord Jesus, thank You, as I get into my car to head to my destination, to recall to memory that You took the wheel to lead me into the path of righteousness.

Remind me, Lord Jesus, thank You, as I hurry to reach my destination, to recall to memory that in Your Word, You say to wait on You.

Remind me, Lord Jesus, thank You, as I fight the traffic, to recall to memory in Your Word, how You fought Satan in the desert.

Remind me, Lord Jesus, thank You, as we pass by a police car, to recall to memory in Your Word, how You speak of Your everlasting protection for me.

Remind me, Lord Jesus, thank You, as we pass by the courthouse, to recall in Your Word: "Judge not lest ye be judged;" that I am a sinner too.

Remind me, Lord Jesus, thank You, as we pass by children playing in the park, to recall to memory in Your Word: "Suffer the little children who come unto Me."

Remind me, Lord Jesus, thank you, when we pass an ambulance rushing to save lives, to recall to memory that it is through You all lives are saved who believe.

Remind me, Lord Jesus, thank You, as we pass by the lake, to recall to memory in Your Word, the story of John the Baptist, who had called people to repent and be baptized in the river Jordan, but when he saw You coming, he said in Matthew 3:13-15: "Then Jesus came from Galilee to John at the river Jordan to be baptized by him. And John tried to prevent Him saying, 'I need to be baptized by You; are You coming to me?' But Jesus answered and said unto him, 'Permit it to be so now, for thus it is fitting for us to fulfill all righteousness.' Then he allowed Him."

Remind me, Lord Jesus, thank You, as we listen to worship music on my car radio, to recall to memory in Your Word, how King David sang his praises to You in the Psalms.

Remind me, Lord Jesus, thank You, when I think I am going to be late, to recall to memory in Your Word that God's timing is perfect!

Remind me, Lord Jesus, thank You, when I become anxious and worried that I won't get to my destination, to recall to memory how in Your Word, You say to "lay all of my cares on You" and trust that You will guide me there.

Remind me, Lord Jesus, thank you, when I think about calling my friends, to recall to memory to call on You, that Your line is always open.

Remind me, Lord Jesus, thank You, when I stop at the bank to pay my tax bill, to recall to memory in Your Word, Matthew, the tax collector who couldn't look upon You, as he knew he was a sinner, yet you called him to be one of the twelve disciples.

Remind me, Lord Jesus, thank You, as we pass by the delivery truck, to recall in the Lord's Prayer: "Deliver us from evil."

Remind me, Lord Jesus, thank You, to recall to memory that any person I happen to meet, I will see only what is good inside of them, as You saw in me.

Remind me, Lord Jesus, thank You, to recall to memory that when anyone makes a mistake toward me, to forgive them as You forgave me.

Remind me, Lord Jesus, thank You, as we pass by the tower, to recall to memory in Your Word, Proverbs 18:10: "The name of the Lord is a strong tower, the righteous run to it and are safe."

Remind me, Lord Jesus, thank You, as we drive by the tower with two flags flying from it, to recall to memory how Jonathan, son of King Saul, and David, who was anointed by You to be king, swore friendship with each other forever before You.

Remind me, Lord Jesus, thank You, as we pass the grocery store, to recall to memory to not forsake the needs of others, as You didn't mine; You have given me everything I need.

Remind me, Lord Jesus, thank You, as we pass the graveyard, to offer comfort to those who are mourning, as Your Holy Spirit comforted me.

Remind me, Lord Jesus, thank You, as we pass by the hot dog stand, to bless the one who prepares the food, to recall to memory in Your Word, how You fed the five thousand.

Remind me, Lord Jesus, thank You, as I write this, to recall to memory that I not seek gain from men in the world, but seek gain from You, who is not of this world.

Remind me, Lord Jesus, thank You, as we reach my destination, to recall to memory that when we get out of the car to go and knock on the door; it was You who opened it for me!

Remind me, Lord Jesus, thank You, that the tasks performed there were successful; not to dare praise myself but offer praise up to You, because without You I can do nothing.

Remind me, Lord Jesus, thank You, to recall to memory that before I came to know You as my Savior, You sent help when I was in trouble, and because of Your unspeakable love for me, You did it without thanks.

Remind me, Lord Jesus, thank You, when someone asks for help even though I'm tired, to do it quickly, as it was really You doing the asking.

Remind me, Lord Jesus, thank You, to recall to memory to share the gifts You gave me, so others may know they are for anyone that asks of them from You.

Remind me, Lord Jesus, thank You, to recall to memory the coat I needed that day to keep warm, and to give the extra one I have to someone who needs one.

Remind me, Lord Jesus, thank You, as I go to the council meeting, to recall to memory that when I'm unsure of anything, to seek council from You, so that whatever I do sees favor with You.

Remind me, Lord Jesus, thank You, to recall to memory to say thank you to others for everything big or small; it was You who did it for me.

Remind me, Lord Jesus, thank You, to recall to memory that whenever I feel down or depressed, to praise You even more, for all the wonderful things in this life and eternally which You have done for me make me feel better.

Remind me, Lord Jesus, thank You, as we pass by the library, to recall to memory to seek in Your Word, Your wisdom.

Remind me, Lord Jesus, thank you, as we see the man wrestling in the alley with another to recall to memory in Your Word, Genesis 32:24-28, how Jacob wrestled with You.

Remind me, Lord Jesus, thank You, as we pass by the broken-hearted woman who was betrayed, to recall to memory that You were betrayed by Judas Iscariot.

Remind me, Lord Jesus, thank You, to recall to memory in Your Word, to help carry others' burdens, that as You carried the cross and fell, Simon of Cyrene helped to carry it for You.

Remind me, Lord Jesus, thank You, as we pass by the hospital where people are sick and dying, to recall in Your Word, how You raised the dead, healed the sick, made the lame man to walk, helped the blind to see, and cured the lepers, among many other miracles You performed.

Remind me, Lord Jesus, thank You, when I see a woman about to give birth, to recall to memory Luke 2:6-7: "And so it was, that, while they were there, the days were accomplished that she should be delivered. And she brought forth her firstborn Son, and wrapped Him in swaddling clothes, and laid Him in a manger, because there was no room at the inn."

Remind me, Lord Jesus, thank You, when the doctor asks how the patient is doing, to recall to memory in Your Word, what the apostle Paul said in Romans 5:3: "And not only so, but we glory in the trials and tribulations also knowing that tribulation worketh patience." KJV

Remind me, Lord Jesus, thank You, as we hit a giant pothole in the road and become afraid, to recall to memory in Your Word the story of the Road to Damascus, where Saul, now the apostle Paul, encountered You.

Remind me, Lord Jesus, thank You, as we pass the school, to recall to memory in Your Word, Proverbs 18:15: 'The heart of the prudent acquires knowledge, and the ear of the wise seek it out."

Remind me, Lord Jesus, thank You, when we stop to attend a town council meeting, to recall to memory in Your Word, Psalm 73:24: 'Thou shalt guide me with thy council, and receive me to glory."

Remind me, Lord Jesus, thank You, that as we pass by the hearing aid clinic, to recall to memory in Your Word, Isaiah 30:21: "Whether you turn your head to the right, or the left, your ears will hear a voice behind you saying, 'This is the way, walk in it.'"

Remind me, Lord Jesus, thank You, as we pass by a wedding that Your greatest commandment was to "love each other as You loved the church."

Remind me, Lord Jesus, thank You, at times when I feel alone and abandoned, to recall to memory in Your Word, John 16:32: "But a time is coming and has come, when you will be scattered, each to his own home. You will leave me all alone. Yet I am not alone, for my Father is with me."

Remind me, Lord Jesus, thank You, as the day has darkened to night, and I have put my headlights on, to recall to memory in Your Word, Genesis 1:4: "And when God saw the light, that it was good: and God divided the light from the darkness."

Remind me, Lord Jesus, thank You, as we arrive home, to think of Heaven, which will someday be my real home.

Remind me, Lord Jesus, thank You, as we prepare supper for our invited guests, to recall to memory in Your Word, Revelations 19:9, in which John wrote: "Then the angel said to me, 'Write: "Blessed are those who are invited to the wedding supper of the Lamb!" And he added, 'These are the true words of God.'"

Remind me, Lord Jesus, thank You, as I rush to get my chores done for the evening, to recall to memory the story of Martha, who was busying herself with chores instead of just being still, and listen to what You have to say, like her sister Mary.

Holy Spirit of Jesus, thank You, as my day is now over and I get ready for bed, remind me to recall to memory in Your Word: Luke 9:58 "but the Son of Man has nowhere to lay His head."

Holy Spirit of Jesus, thank You. I don't need to be reminded of what is said in Your Word, Matthew 6:9-13: "After this manner therefore pray ye:
'Our Father which art in heaven,
Hallowed be thy name.
Thy kingdom come,
Thy will be done in earth, as it is in heaven.
Give us this day our daily bread.
And forgive us our debts,
As we forgive our debtors.
And lead us not into temptation,
But deliver us from evil:
For thine is the kingdom, and the power and the glory,
   for ever.
Amen.'"

Jesus, If I Had To

Jesus, if I had to do it all again,
I would have listened and not complained.
I know that You are faithful and always true,
No one knows my heart, only You.
All the years spent running away,
Now to You I run everyday.
Jesus, if I had to do it all again,
I'd have looked to You to take away my pain.
To smash out the darkness of night,
And brought sin forward to Your glorious light.
All of my sins I would've sooner confessed,
Given You all of my brokenness.
Jesus, if I had to do it all again,
Every sentence from my mouth would have been Amen.
My children would have known real love and faith,
Would have known worldly ambitions are nothing but fake.
Would have accepted Your Spirit as their friend,
That stayed with them to the very end.
Jesus, if I had to do it all again,
Would have known there was no one to take the blame.
Would have followed You to the ends of the earth,
Studied all my life in Your Spirit's Word.
Would have been a better friend, wife and mother,
Would have called everyone sister or brother.

Jesus, if I had to do it all again,
I wouldn't be thinking I'd never change.
And toward others have a softer heart,
Dear Lord Jesus, where do I start?
I've tried so hard many times,
To be part of that fruitful vine.
Jesus, if I had to do it all again,
Wouldn't have led a life full of shame.
Given to the poor as much as I could,
Would have known now where I stood.
Would have tried to help the next generation,
Preaching Your life giving Salvation.
"Dear Child,
If I had to do it all again,
I wouldn't have changed a thing!"
Amen

Searching

The heart cries out for its first love,
That's as innocent as a dove.
Searching all through the Holy pages,
To find that love of all the ages.
It looked in the beginning of creation,
And found the beginning of all the world's nations.
The heart bleeds to find where it belongs,
Longing to find its true home.
It's never satisfied with things of this world,
It looks in the east, then in the west, south and north.
So on and on through the pages it searches,
Roams through the halls of ancient first churches.
Learns the coming of its affection,
And waits for its Love's final inspection.
It looks from Old Testament to the New,
Suddenly finds hope in the pages of Matthew,
Learning the birth of this heart's Master.
The chest in which the heart is stored,
Fiercely beats to be restored.
Now in the pages it feels the Master not far off,
Tracing His footsteps, which are light and soft.
Throughout the pages it hears His voice,
The heart beats harder, begins to rejoice!
Jumping from page to page, it continues searching,

For the One who quenches the heart's thirsting.
But the search must go on as the heart now knows,
This is the only true love it will ever know.
But now its Love, it learned, has a name,
"Jesus," it cries out on this special page.
In recognition it had long ago known,
It heard the Spirit say "One day you'll be home!"
Seeing the Object of its search through the eyes of its windows.
Making the heart beat to Heaven's crescendo.
Oh, what a day, what a beautiful day,
Its Master has come to take it away.
The search now over, with its love, Jesus,
Who restored the heart of all its broken pieces!

Miracle At Melaren's Creek

It was already December 1st, and things were in full swing preparing for Christmas! Shoppers at the malls, running to get the sales, stores prettily decorated getting ready for the last-minute Christmas rush. Children were coming in to visit the mall Santa with cheer and excitement, telling him all they wished for Christmas.

"Oh, it's so festive and beautiful!" said Anna but to her Christmas was never the same after her children left home. Everything inside her told her that this was life, and she had to accept it, but the more she rationalized this, the more resentful she became, so no, she was not having Christmas this year!,

"Why am I behaving this way?" Anna thought bitterly to herself. "I've loved Christmas all my life! Why do things have to change!" She wept to herself. "I wish my children knew how much I missed them, especially at this time of year."

Anna was not a Christian woman. She did believe in God and even Jesus, but for everybody else, not for her. She foolishly believed over the years that you could only depend on yourself, period! And she never sought to pray to Him. *What's the use? He never listens!* she thought. As a child, Anna felt alone; even with siblings she felt she just didn't belong. Then Anna had two daughters, Julie and

Kirsten. She thought she would never be alone again, they would always be there, not taking into account that one day, they would grow up and have lives of their own.

During a recent visit, the girls asked, "Mom, why haven't you put up your Christmas decorations? You always put them up." Anna loved decorating for Christmas the most.

"Oh, I'm just too tired to be bothered this year," Anna lied, feeling ashamed that she had done so. *How can I tell them how I really feel? They're both so happy and excited about their own plans, I can't spoil it for them,* Anna thought sadly to herself. They were not going to be there, anyway. Anna knew in her heart she was just being selfish, so she dismissed her feelings and went on with the rest of her day.

Soon it was Dec. 23rd, her day to spend Christmas with her daughters, so she busied herself getting dinner ready for them. The girls arrived with smiling faces, telling each other their plans for Christmas Day. All through the day, Anna fought with her emotions. Fighting her tears, she hoped her daughters couldn't see what she was feeling, and thankfully they didn't seem to. Soon it was time for Julie and Kirsten to leave and meet up with their husbands and children that evening. As they were leaving, Anna decided to follow them part way in her car to visit with her friend Elizabeth for the rest of the evening. The weather had changed; it had snowed quite heavily, and the sudden thaw caused McLaren's Creek to overflow with the water running through in torrents. *Hmm, the roads are pretty slippery,* Anna thought to herself as she was driving. *Thank goodness the girls don't have far to drive to get to the main highway*. The highways were well maintained, especially at this time of year.

Just as she was slowing to turn the corner, Anna watched in horror as she saw Julie's car spin out of control and then plunge into the icy waters of McLaren's Creek. Anna screamed, "No, this can't be happening!" She jumped out of her car and ran to the creek where she saw that Julie's car was almost completely submerged. She could hear her precious daughters screaming for help. "Mom! Mom! Help us!" they were screaming. Instantly, Anna dove into the icy waters to save them. She could see the girls were trapped and unable to get their doors open, so she pulled as hard as she could to open the doors. Fear and panic gripped Anna, as she could not get them open.

"Mommy! Please save us!" screamed Kirsten, her youngest daughter. Anna dove under the water to try and get a rock to break the windows, but the current was too strong and she almost lost her grip on the car.

At that moment, Anna realized her daughters' screams were weakening. "No! No! Please God, help me! Don't let them die!" There was a sickening silence as Anna could not hear her daughters' screams anymore, and they weren't struggling to free themselves. "No! This is not happening!" a panic-stricken Anna yelled to herself, still struggling to free her daughters. With a deafening scream and Anna weakening herself, she begged the Lord to give her strength to free her daughters. At that moment, she heard the voice of a stranger. He gave her what looked like a spike and ordered her to use the spike to break the windows. Without thinking, Anna did what she was told, and with all the strength she had left, she hit the window, but nothing happened.

"I can't!" she screamed. "I need your help!"

"Hit it again!" the stranger commanded. As she hit it one last time, the glass shattered, and Anna lost consciousness . . .

"Anna, Anna, can you hear me?" a faint voice called. "Anna, open your eyes, please!" Anna struggled to open her eyes. It was her husband Mike and her friend Elizabeth.

"Where am?" she said weakly.

"Anna, you're in the hospital," said Mike, fighting back tears at what had happened. Suddenly, panic and fear struck Anna. "The girls! Where are the girls?" she cried, as she struggled to get up. The doctor helped Mike to gently lower Anna to the bed.

"You have to rest, Mrs. Maxwell."

Mike, heart-broken for both himself and his wife, told her the girls were there and the situation wasn't looking too good for them.

"John and Mark are with them right now," said Elizabeth. John and Mark were Julie's and Kirsten's husbands. Mike left Anna briefly to check on their daughters, so Elizabeth began to tell Anna that Mike and Brian—Elizabeth's husband, who worked with Mike as a fellow paramedic— were just returning home from work when they saw the accident. They, too, had jumped into the water to rescue Anna and the girls. "If you hadn't broken that back window when you did, Anna, the girls wouldn't have stood a chance," said Elizabeth.

Suddenly Anna remembered the stranger who had given her the spike. "Elizabeth," said Anna, "where is the person who gave me the spike?"

"Anna, there was no one else there," said Elizabeth, thinking Anna was just in shock from the injuries she sustained jumping into the river.

"Elizabeth, Doctor, I need to go see my girls. Please let me go see them!"

"I'm afraid we can't, Mrs. Maxwell. You've broken your neck and sustained injuries to your heart. I've given you something to help you rest. Your daughters are in good hands, trust me."

Soon Anna was once again unconscious. "Anna," a voice called out. "Anna . . ." the gentle voice called again, and this time Anna opened her eyes. There he was, the stranger who had given her the spike. Anna could feel a strange presence about her, but was too weak to ask questions. All she wanted was to see her daughters. "Anna," the stranger said, "I'm going to take you to them." Gently lifting her broken body in his arms, he took her to where her girls were.

As she lifted her head, she saw her daughters' husbands weeping beside their wives' beds, praying to God to save them. They seemed unaware that she and the stranger were there. As she looked upon the seemingly lifeless bodies of her daughters, Anna asked the stranger to let her down. Not realizing she had been healed, she fell to her knees and prayed like never before. She pleaded with God in the name of Jesus to spare the lives of her children and to take hers instead. She confessed she was unworthy to ask anything of Him, and also, she hadn't prayed to Him in a long time. The stranger moved toward where her daughters were, and whispered to both of them. Slowly, they opened their eyes. "Mommy!" Kirsten cried.

"Mom," said Julie weakly. "You saved us."

Anna, overcome with joy, ran to her daughters and hugged them both. "I didn't save you, this stranger did," Anna said, not knowing His name. "He gave me a spike to break the window!" said Anna, struggling to remember what had happened.

"No, Mom," Julie said, "Jesus said your faith saved us. You asked for His help to save us and then took the spike without question! You see, Mom, Jesus told us He hadn't heard from you in a very long time; in fact, since you were a little girl, and then He told us He missed you, especially at Christmas!"

Anna, not realizing she had been healed, fell to her knees and begged Jesus to forgive her and thanked Him for sparing the lives of her daughters. She stood up also to thank the stranger, but when He reached out His hands, Anna suddenly noticed there were holes in them. It was then that Anna realized the stranger was Jesus!

"You have to go now, Mom," said her daughters tearfully but happily, as Jesus promised them He would take good care of her and that He would make sure their father Mike would be okay.

"Welcome home Anna. I've really missed you, especially at Christmas!" said the Lord.

Amen.

Jesus Showed Me

Life threw me a curveball,
Jesus turned it into a home run.
The world showed me a life without Jesus,
Jesus showed me a life with Him.
The world gave me tears of sorrow,
Jesus gave me tears of joy.
The world held me in darkness,
Jesus lifted me to His light.
The world showed me weakness and fear,
Jesus showed me strength and courage.
The world showed me hate and diversity,
Jesus showed me love and unity.
The world showed me unforgiveness and sickness,
Jesus showed me healing and forgiveness.
The world laid upon me the heaviest of burdens,
Jesus told me He'd take the weight.
The world condemned me,
Jesus saved me.
The world left me drowning in troubled waters,
But Jesus left me beside still waters.
The world demanded perfection,
But Jesus took me as I am.
The world demanded everything I had,
But Jesus showed me He was all I needed.

The world taught me shadowy knowledge that bore me nothing,
But Jesus taught me heavenly things, through the power of His written Word of the Holy Spirit.
The world showed me lies and deceit,
Jesus showed me truth and valor,
The world showed me how to curse,
Jesus taught me how to pray.
The world showed me weapons of mass destruction,
But Jesus showed me the whole armor of God.
The world showed me battles to be fought,
Jesus showed me battles already won.
The world showed me to be nothing but cross,
Jesus told me to bring it all to the cross.
The world showed me storms coming,
But Jesus walked me through them.
The world taught me how to say thank you,
But Jesus showed me saying thank you for His sacrifice on the cross, would never be enough.
The world taught me foolishness,
But Jesus showed me His foolishness was wiser than any scholar.
The world taught me all good things come to an end,
But Jesus taught me His goodness was just the beginning.
When the world taught me to reflect on my shortcomings,
Jesus taught me to reflect on His coming.
The world taught me its strength would fail,
But Jesus taught me His strength would, no matter what, prevail.
The world showed me loneliness,

Jesus gave me His Holy Spirit to be my friend.
The world showed me its debilitating pride,
But Jesus showed me His beautiful humility.
The world showed me death, destruction and sin,
Jesus showed me signs, wonders and miracles!
Amen

Nails

As I knelt at the cross like others before me,
To remove those nails, I could only weep.
Your broken body caused my heart to quiver,
Your sinless life traded for 30 pieces of silver.
To see those nails that I and others saw,
Holding You painfully on that wooden cross,
Took away my life, took away my breath,
To see the crown of thorns, I deserved death.
Lord, it was more than we could bear,
Let us remove those nails and wash Your blood-soaked hair.
Our souls reached for the nails but were stopped,
Because of the promise You made with God.
Those nails pierced like a sickening laugh,
Were not letting go till You'd seen Your last.
We tried to grab those nails of sin,
But were held by Your Spirit's mighty wind.
We were helpless, as every attempt failed,
To take back what should have been our sin-filled nails.
Then a voice in the wind gently called,
"This was planned since Adam and Eve's dreadful fall.
Those nails you see, are meant for me,
For every sin, there was a need.
I forged those nails to be your Deliverer,
Yes, planned My betrayal with those pieces of silver.

They were forged to mend all broken hearts,
To give My children a brand-new start.
The nails of my hands, were the proof I needed,
To show the world, like Thomas, My plan succeeded.
Children no longer cry, but rejoice,
I've beaten sin; it no longer has a voice.
I was raised from the dead,
And now I live,
My life for all was my choice to give.
Until the Father's specified time,
Those nails will remain always mine.
Take up Your gifts that were Heaven sent,
Like others before you, write what I've said.
And speak of those nails so others repent,
With My Spirit's paper, desk and a pen."
Amen

Lampstand

This lampstand held high burns warm and bright,
Given by the Lord Jesus, His Holy light.
Proudly it sits, waiting for someone to shine through,
Out of the darkness full of life and His truth.
The willowing flicker from above,
Beckons the soul of its true love.
The lampstand is carefully given and carefully placed,
By the Lord Jesus for everyone to embrace.
However, the lampstand's light has become low,
Its beauty slowly forgotten from long ago.
Its caregiver has left it all alone,
Not knowing Jesus was taking it home.
He took it to someone who wouldn't neglect,
Giving the lampstand to His elect.
Its previous owner looks for the lampstand,
But Jesus found someone, was it woman or a man?
The terrified cry from the fallen soul,
Begs the Lord to give back that warming glow!
This is what Jesus said:
"The lampstand now belongs to someone else,
But if you repent, there's another in My house.
There are many lampstands that need to be held,
To be kept brightly lit, saving others from hell.
You had forgotten the light of your lamp,

And so it was that I took it and sorely wept.
So, carefully and joyfully take the lampstand in hand,
Love it and others is my command.
This lampstand, forever, I will see it shine,
Others I've given, but this one is Mine.
Remember in my Spirit's Holy written Word,

Revelations 2:5
'Remember therefore from where you have fallen;
repent and do the first works, or else I will come to you
 quickly and remove your lampstand from its place,
 unless you repent.'"
Amen

Competition

There were two friends, you see,
They both wanted life and to be free.
They wanted their sins forgiven and erased,
They longed to see Jesus face to face.
One friend went to church so he could repent,
The other bowed down with knees humbly bent.
Each one professing their love and respect,
Anything not of the Lord they would reject.
Each shared miracles the Lord had given,
Sharing their joy, knowing they were forgiven.
Each day they prayed to Jesus our King,
Each day together praises they'd sing!
Till one day pride set in one's heart,
Whose prayer would it be that hit its mark?
His friend so confident smiled and walked away,
While the other asked the Lord, why had this come their way?
The friend, he worshipped confident and unafraid,
He was going to win this prayerful crusade.
His prayers were impressive to say the least,
Certain his prayers could slay any beast.
The other sat down with paper and pen,
A letter to the Lord lovingly said:
Dear Lord Jesus, examine my heart,
This competition I want to depart.

I love you, Lord, but I'm broken and torn,
Sin got in, as You had warned.
This had surprised me, I didn't know,
That this was the way some things would go.
Deliver my friend from envy and pride,
Deliver my hurt that's deep inside.
All I have is this paper and pen,
And simple words that come from within.
I love my friend so please let him win,
Thank you, Lord Jesus, and Amen.

Missing

As I go about my busy day,
Wondering, Jesus, what You'd have to say.
Lord, my work is busy as my mind wanders,
Are You really with me, in the rain, lightning and thunder?
I train my heart to try and listen,
Knowing this busy day, it's You I'm missing.
I think of the day that You had called me,
You opened my heart with Your holy key.
Now the sun, the moon, the things of the earth,
Are nothing to me when I think of You first.
Lord, as I wash, dry, and fold all my laundry,
All through the task, it's You I'm missing.
The days are short, the night is long,
I can't wait to read the Book of Psalms.
My heart looks to You and Your Spirit's Word,
That when I read my spirit is stirred.
As I busy myself with daily chores,
Through them all, it's You I'm missing.
Your love for us I can never comprehend,
Thinking of all the hearts You've had to mend.
When I listen to prophetic worship music, I sing,
I'm lifted to Heaven with Your Spirit's anointing.
Once again I'm brought down to earthly prison,
Not wanting to fit in, Jesus, it's You I'm missing.

While I drive to the store, I think of what it means,
To walk in the fullness of the Spirit so serene!
Tears fill the saddened eyes,
As we ponder and ponder and wonder why,
How did we get here and get so lost?
The ugliness of this world is not worth the cost.
As I drive home tired and reminiscing,
My heart screams, Jesus, it's You I'm missing!
All through these busy and hurried seasons,
I remember the day I started believing,
You broke the chains and set me free.
Expectations ran high as now I see,
The beauty of You, on bended knees,
With aching tears that constantly flow.
How wonderful you are the more I grow.
Jesus, I can't pray these fancy words,
Can't remember Scripture, that's for sure.
But one thing I try to do is listen,
To that still, small voice that tells me it's You I'm missing!
I pray an end comes to this busy day,
Cause at Your feet I'd rather stay.
Lord, forgive my humble complaint,
It's hard to know You and not want to faint.
Your love fills my heart, it just aches,
Knowing in this life I'll just have to wait.
Till one day I'll just stop always wishing,
Cause I'll be with You and no longer missing.
Amen

Unwavering

Lord of my heart,
Where do I start?
I opened Your Word,
And soon I had learned,
It is Your Holy Spirit
That supplies our gifts,
To heal, to comfort and to uplift!
He descended over Jesus like a dove,
Delivering into us all of Your love.
Oh Lord, keep pouring that love into me,
Never have I tasted anything so sweet.
You want my heart and love more than anything else,
Wholeheartedness is what You're after, the Bible tells.
Then let me be the first sinner that stands in line,
To let the gift of Your love now in me shine!
Jesus, I mess up each and every day,
But I will continue running the race.
The gift of Your love helps me to pray,
Till one day, Jesus, we meet face to face.
I've tasted the sickening other side of life,
Its bitterness is dark, there is no light.
Lord, not in a second could I ever go back,
The very thought turns my mind black!
I know what it's like to be far from You,

My blood ran cold, missing You.
Oh Lord, thy God, Your Majesty,
How do I ever really thank thee?
For giving me life,
And a strong will to fight,
So when the powers of hell come up against me,
I'm no longer afraid; up against You they flee.
Your children from Your hand they will never snatch,
Your unwavering love just can't be matched!
Amen! And thank You, Lord!

Written by Pat Davis
Given by The Holy Spirit!

Jesus And The Swimmer

The swimmer was ready or so he thought,
Thoughts of negativity, he had surely fought.
He swam through the pages of love's perfect light,
He swam through the pages of the darkest nights.
Through the underwater caverns and the darkened caves,
He discovered the Living Waters and it's cooling waves.
Taking in the Spirit's pureness of breath,
Escaped the muddied waters of certain death.
Jesus smiled lovingly, as the swimmer prayed,
Telling Him he'd practiced each and every day.
He swam the smooth waters with a stroke of a pen,
Out to the deep, and then back again.
"Jesus, I've studied hard, honed in on my skills,
Swam the waters of brokenness, learning of Your sacrifice
    on Calvary's Hill."
Jesus smiled and lovingly said,
"This unfamiliar pool is where you'll swim instead."
"It's okay, Jesus," the swimmer replied,
"I have Your Holy Spirit, right by my side!"
The swimmer made his way to the unfamiliar pool,
Surely he would conquer; he'd studied in Heaven's school.
The swimmer was ready to dive right in,
This pool held uncertainty, it's waters murky from within.
Slowly he entered, unsure of himself,

What would he find, what was this about?
At first it seemed shallow, easy to swim,
Easy on mind, body and limb.
The waters became deeper, uneasy to see,
Waves of doubt swept him out to sea.
It's swells of confusion filled the swimmer with dread,
Each stroke became harder, putting his skills to the test.
He could only make it halfway at best,
He needed his Savior's help, and His holy rest.
"Holy Spirit of Jesus!" he cried out for help.
All that he knew, he just wanted out.
Sinking beneath the deep waters of despair,
Uncertain the Holy Spirit would meet him there.
The swimmer looked up, unable to breathe,
When suddenly the hand of Jesus
Lifted him out of the sea.
Jesus laid the swimmer in the warmth of His robe,
Breathing him life until he awoke.
"Savior, forgive me!" he cried in tear-soaked clothes.
"I failed the test, no more will I boast!"
Jesus wiped gently the swimmer's brow,
With Salvation's saving blood-stained towel.
This was His plan from the beginning of creation,
For every man, woman, and child,
From each and every nation!
Amen

Jesus Was There

The waters were quiet, calm and very still,
We were naïve, and lacked mariner skills.
The waters beckoned, "It's okay, just come right through."
Its color oh-so bright, shiny and coral blue!
We plunged our vessel into the water's allure,
Unaware of what we would eventually endure.
Gliding through silvery waters with wisps of cooling sprays,
Our destination we'll meet at the end of this day.
For a while we were accompanied by flocks of squawking
    birds,
While splashes of gentle waves were its only words.
Floating along without ever a care,
All was well, as we knew Jesus was there.
Sailing for hours we had soon realized,
No land could we see with instruments or eyes.
Our vessel's navigation had cruelly failed,
Our radio out of range so no one could we hail.
We didn't know our vessel's northerly direction,
We couldn't make any course corrections.
Terrified and lost in laughing, unfriendly waters,
Panic became my heart's nightmarish scoffer.
"Lord," I fearfully cried, "help us find our way,
Show us a sign, the skies are turning grey!"
As we looked to east then to the west,

With the sun dying down, it was hard to see anything at best.
A far-off vessel caught the navigator's eye,
With night closing in we were almost blind.
But the navigator, he stayed right on the vessel's course,
Steering toward it sent by the Lord.
We were finally in the channel close to land,
Safety was getting closer, surely at hand.
Cheering in my heart, we thought we'd made it,
When one of our vessels' engines woefully quit.
The strong, unscrupulous currents were dragging us back,
Now by this time in my mind everything went black.
The navigator tried to restart our vessel's failed engine,
But another vessel appeared, headed we were into a collision!
Quickly he steered the vessel to the right; he saw a vacant dock,
With the current being so strong, I thought all was lost.
Then suddenly a voice from nowhere yelled, "Do you need any help?"
"Yes," I cried, "we've no navigation, one of our engines is out."
"Try to get your vessel over here!" the commanding voice cried,
"Come to the dock that's under the light!"
We were led to the Coast Guard; this was not just luck,
This was the Lord's doing, was all I could deduct!
The navigator struggled to bring the vessel in,
Till finally the battle with the current he would win.
They quickly guided us safely to the well-lit dock,
While I tried to comprehend this overwhelming shock.

Guiding me keenly to throw our vessel's ropes,
While they tried to calm the nerves of this terrified
    worn-out soul.
With a warm cup of coffee, their kindness was shown,
Jesus proved to us we were not alone.
They proceeded to tell us how lucky we were,
The biggest storm ever should have occurred.
Jesus had guided us back all the way home,
Knowing we would sail into the unknown.
He took us both right back to where we had started,
All along at our helm we were safely guarded.
The Lord knew the vessel needed repair,
And you know, after all we had been through,
With a sigh of relief we knew,
Jesus was there.
Amen!

Based on actual events!

Call Out To Jesus

When life comes crashing in like a tidal wave,
Call out to Jesus!
When the night has come to take away the day,
Call out to Jesus!
When the pain threatens to overtake you,
Call out to Jesus!
When brokenness has become too much,
Call out to Jesus!
When you feel despair overtaking you,
Call out to Jesus!
When you feel loneliness has been your company too long,
Call out to Jesus!
When the hurt has been so great you can't forgive,
Call out to Jesus!
When love has died and bitterness holds you,
Call out to Jesus!
When you think you just can't go another mile,
Call out to Jesus!
When fear has its grip on your heart,
Call out to Jesus!
When you feel lost with nowhere to go,
Call out to Jesus!
When you feel the world has passed you by,
Call out to Jesus!

When illness has got a hold of you,
Call out to Jesus!
When you're drowning in the river of tears,
Call out to Jesus!
When loss has seemed so great,
Call out to Jesus!
When you have no one to share with,
Call out to Jesus!
When you feel hopeless and confused,
Call out to Jesus!
When this world of sin might overtake you,
Call out to Jesus!
When you're losing the love of your life,
Call out to Jesus!
When it smashes the breath right out of you,
Call out to Jesus!
When you find yourself with nothing to cling to,
Call out to Jesus!
When the nights seem like they will never end,
Call out to Jesus!
When you long to hear the voice of your loved one,
Call out to Jesus!
When death is near, and you've nothing left,
Call out Jesus!
When all is lost that you ever hoped for,
Call out to Jesus!
When you're looking for someone to love you,
Call out to Jesus!
When you've nothing left to give,
Call out to Jesus!

When you don't know where to go,
Call out to Jesus!
When sorrow tries to take your life,
Call out to Jesus!
If your faith is waning,
Call out to Jesus!
If you find you want to go home to Heaven,
Call out to Jesus!
If you find your emotions threatening to hold you forever in darkness,
Call out to Jesus!
When you need understanding,
Call out to Jesus!
When you need that smile,
Call out to Jesus!
When you need that hug,
Call out to Jesus!
If you find that you've lost all strength,
Call out to Jesus!
And when you just need a friend to talk to,
Call out to Jesus!
If you find you're having trouble calling out to the Lord,
Call out to Jesus!
Jesus:
"When you call out to Me, I will answer.
You will find that in all these times of life, I am right by your side, loving, healing, walking, carrying, talking with you,
And through it all, I will bring you through.
Love, Jesus"
Amen

Tears From A Pen

The writer sits at the old desk,
Contemplating what he would write as he picks up the pen.
He takes some scraps of old paper preparing what he'll say,
Before writing, he bows his head and begins to pray.
"I want this story to be about You, Lord," he weeps.
"Let the words written be for everyone who is asleep.
The world You know has spun out of control,
I pray, Lord, that whatever is written will reach every
 broken soul.
There are so many who don't know how truly wonderful
 You are,
You suffered the anger of hell and to Heaven carried its
 scars.
I know there are many books about You written,
Awe! Your Word; if one reads about You, will become
 smitten.
You have captured the broken, blackened heart of sin,
To enter the refining fire to cleanse from within.
The world once a chasm of Your wonderful creation,
Now corrupt and death in each and every nation.
But when I think of You and pick up this pen,
All I see is the beauty of Your love and of Heaven.
It is not an easy road to travel but if I have to I will crawl,

Scraps of Old Paper, a Desk and a Pen

So let me take up this pen; let it be Your Words not mine
  that are scrawled."
The writer completes his prayer,
Straightens himself up in his chair.
In silence he sits, waiting for the Lord, feeling completely
  drained,
With swollen eyes, yet a smile replaces the pain.
Slowly he picks up the paper and pen,
Preparing to write what he hears from within.
He leans over his desk and begins to write,
The pen wrote tears, beautiful and contrite.
Every drop spoke to his heart and the heart of every man,
"I am Jesus," it wrote, "keep this pen in hand."
Tears flowed from the writer's pen,
The writer wondering what they all meant.
The writer, overtaken from what had been written,
His face glowed with joy reading the composition.
Now understanding God's love throughout his years,
The tears from the pen mixed with his tears.
You see the tears from the pen were the Lord's,
They filled every ocean of all the world's shores.
He wrote tears of how He loved all from the cross,
He wrote tears of mankind and how much they have lost.
He wrote in tears calling man to come near,
He holds all in His heart that hold Him dear!
The tears from the pen gently flowed
As it is man's will, some He has to let go.
Oh, how if we chose Him He could save us all,
Pleading for man to heed the voice of His call.
"Love Me and others," His tears ever wanted.

"Forgiveness and love for all is My final offer!
My Holy Spirit I give to see you through,
He will comfort and heal, revealing secrets of Me to you.
Tears of the forgiven in My cup I've collected,
Through My sacrifice if you repent, you'll be perfected.
Man, the cheap and fake powers of this world,
If you continue to follow will send you to hell.
Run, run to Me while you still can,
For I am coming soon to take up the tears from My pen."
The writer fell asleep but ended with tears of Amen and Amen.

Epilogue

If you've read this book, you can see how Jesus has been there in every instance. This book is fiction based on fact that describes the struggles in life we all face. But as we look back on our lives, if we are willing, we'll see that no matter what, when we call on the Lord for help, He is always there even when we don't know it!

My life has changed so dramatically that as I sit here writing this, I never thought in a million years that I would become an author through the Lord. Never did I think I could be of any value to Him. As a matter of fact, I asked, "What could I possibly do for You?"

Turns out, a lot!

My journey has only just begun and I have a long way to go, but in the end the very thought of "being in the trenches" with Jesus (as our Reverend Brent calls it), excites me, as we await His glorious return—and that others will be saved and serve in ways they never thought possible! When Jesus calls you to follow Him, you will find yourself saying a resounding "Yes!" and wanting to do it over and over again, while hanging on for the ride of your life!

Amen!

Printed in the USA
CPSIA information can be obtained
at www.ICGtesting.com
LVHW090741040824
787305LV00009B/495